La Lechuza

Tales from the Graveyard Series

An Extreme-Horror Short Story

Written by

Wade H. Garrett

V4

WARNING!

WARNING: This book is extreme and contains filthy, grotesque, and brutal torture scenes. It contains GRAPHIC CONTENT, ADULT LANGUAGE, & POLITICAL INCORRECTNESS, may be disturbing to sensitive readers, and should only be read by the seasoned extreme-horror reader.

Front cover illustration by:

Wade H. Garrett

Edited by:

Richard Eckert

Proofread by:

JR Coker

Missy Mayhem

Ozy Von Schrecken

Summary:

This is a spinoff story from the book *The Gravedigger* and loosely based on a true story. Thiago Martinez, an abuser and drunk, comes to realize La Lechuza, a mythical creature in Mexican folklore, is much more than just a fable. A gripping supernatural story with a touch of extreme horror.

Contents

The Owl Witch

On a Wednesday shortly after 3 PM, a taxi pulled up to an old house in Rosevine, Texas, an unincorporated community in northwestern Sabine County in Texas. Thiago Angel Martinez, a stocky fifty-year-old man with a bald head, large mustache, and covered in tattoos, slipped the driver a sweaty wad of cash, then strolled up to the front door. Finding it locked, frustration came over him as he pounded on it with the side of his fist. "It's me, Thiago! Open the pinche puerta (fucking door)!"

A middle-aged woman opened the door. Her eyes grew huge as a worried expression came over her. Thiago wrapped his arms around his wife and pulled her tight. "Big Daddy is home!" Twelve years ago, Thiago struck a SUV while driving drunk and killed four people: a father, mother, their thirteen-year-old son, and eight-year-old daughter. Between the four counts of intoxication manslaughter and his fifth DWI, the judge sentenced him to twenty years in prison. After serving twelve years in Texas State

Penitentiary in Huntsville, Texas, he was released early for good behavior.

Being in an abusive marriage for the last eighteen years, Maria not only felt no emotions toward Thiago, but she was also frightened of him. "Sorry, T. I didn't know you were getting out today. I would have picked you up."

"It's all good, baby. I wanted to surprise you." He glanced over her shoulder. "Where's Diego?" Diego was Thiago's seventeen-year-old son."

"He's still at school."

"Good. I need some panocha."

She pushed away from him. "Maybe later. Diego will be home soon."

As he followed her into the house, he grumbled, "Come on, baby. I've been locked up for a long time."

"I said maybe later."

He shoved her toward a hallway. "Get your ass in the bedroom, woman."

Worried Thiago would become upset, she did as instructed. Fifteen minutes later, Thiago strolled into the kitchen butt naked and opened the refrigerator. His entire body from his neck to his feet showcased gang-related and prison style tattoos. "Where's the cerveza?"

Sitting on the edge of the bed distraught, Maria remained quiet.

"I asked you a fuckin' question!"

"We don't have any."

He glanced inside a cabinet where he kept his liquor. "Where in the fuck is my tequila?"

"I threw it out after you were arrested."

The thought of Maria having an affair crossed his mind. He stormed into the bedroom and glared at her. "Have you been fuckin' someone while I've been locked up!?!"

"Of course, not. Why would you think that?"

"You're actin' guilty."

"I can't believe you're accusing me of something like that. All I've done in the last twelve years is worked my ass off to keep up with the bills since you weren't around."

In a fit of rage, he grasped her by the hair and jerked her to the feet. "What the fuck did you say to me, you fuckin' puta!?!"

"Please let go! I didn't mean anything by it!"

The front door opened and slammed shut. "Who in the fuck is that?"

"It's Diego. Please let go of me before he sees us."

Thiago shoved her onto the bed right as Diego approached the doorway. When he saw his mother's terrified expression and his father's nude body, confusion swept over him. "What's going on?"

Thiago frowned. "Glad to see you too, Son."

Diego, an easygoing teen with a normally mild temperament, scowled when he spotted his mother's smeared mascara. "What did you do to my mom, asshole?"

"You need to watch your mouth, boy. And I'll deal with your ass in a minute." Thiago slammed the door shut.

Anger consumed Diego as he stood in the hallway. "If you touch her, I'll fuckin' kill you!"

A few minutes later, Thiago jerked the door open wearing blue jeans, a red and black buffalo-plaid shirt, a red banana, and white Nike Cortez sneakers. "You ain't gonna threaten me in my house, punk."

Knowing his father possessed a violent temper, Diego muttered as he stomped toward his bedroom. "I wish you would have never gotten out. We made it just fine without your ass."

"What the fuck did you say, ese!?!"

He slammed his door shut.

"You better start showin' me some fuckin' respect, boy! Or you can get the fuck out of my house!" Agitated, Thiago marched into his own bedroom. "Give me the keys to your truck?"

Maria really didn't care if Thiago got arrested for driving with a suspended driver's license, a violation of his parole, or if he got drunk and killed himself, but she didn't want anyone else to get hurt. "I can drive you, so you don't get in trouble."

"I'm a grown fuckin' man. I can drive myself. Give me your fuckin' keys."

Worried he would become aggressive, she grabbed her purse sitting on top of a dresser. Thiago snatched it from her hands and began digging around. After he found her keys, he opened her wallet and pulled out a wad of cash.

"I need that to pay the rent."

"Fuck the rent." He flung the purse at her, and as he walked out the door, he added, "And don't fuckin' wait up."

Thiago drove Maria's 1978 single-cab Ford pickup straight to El Borracho, a local beer joint about five miles away.

Around 11:30 PM, an old Hispanic man came into the bar as Mexican music played in the background. "Cuyo Ford 78 es el que hay en el estacionamiento (Whose 78 Ford is in the parking lot)?"

Hearing someone inquiring about his truck, Thiago cautiously eyed the man as he sat at the bar counter intoxicated. "You wanna buy it? It's for sale."

The man plopped down next to him on a stool, then placed a rope with seven knots and a jar filled with spices on the countertop. "El diablo viene por ti, señor (The devil is coming for you, sir)."

Thiago scrutinized the items, then glanced at the man, noticing he appeared to be in his eighties, wore tattered clothes, and a large crucifix hung from his beaded necklace. "What do you mean the fuckin' devil is comin' for me?"

"Estoy tratando de ayudarte, señor (I'm trying to help you, sir)."

"Vete a la mierda (Fuck off). I don't need your help. And what are you, some kind of curandero?" A curandero, also known as a folk healer, practices spiritual healing and has the ability to ward off curses and hexes using traditional herbs, remedies, and prayer.

The old man slid the rope and jar next to Thiago, then spoke in broken English. "If you see la vieja bruja (the old witch), you must use these and recite the Canticle of Mary."

"See who?"

"La Lechuza (the owl). I saw her by your truck."

Thiago's eyes narrowed. "What the hell are you talkin' about, old man?"

"La Lechuza, you know, the owl witch."

"I don't believe in that shit."

"You need to heed my warning. La vieja bruja is coming for you."

"That's just a fairytale to scare little niños (kids)."

The old man shoved the rope and jar closer to Thiago. "Como quieras (Suit yourself)." He slipped off his barstool. "Buena suerte, señor (Good luck, mister)."

"I don't need any of your luck."

As the old man left the bar, Thiago eyed the bartender as he shook his head. "Who was that crazy bastard?"

The bartender, a burly Hispanic man, shrugged his shoulders as he wiped a glass with a towel. "Not sure. I've never seen him before."

Thiago shoved the rope and jar across the countertop. "You can throw that shit away."

"Naw, man. I don't want no part of that maldición malvada (evil curse)."

"Don't tell me you believe in that silly shit too."

"I grew up hearing the stories about Lechuza from my grandfather. It scared the hell out of me when I was a niño pequeño (little kid)."

According to centuries-old folklore, villagers burned a woman at the stake for practicing white magic. From the ashes, she arose, transformed into a dreadful creature— a large barn owl with the wretched face of an old crone. La Lechuza, as she was known, became a nocturnal specter, haunting the earth, seeking retribution against the wicked under the cover of darkness. "I heard the same shit when I was a kid. I think our abuelos (grandparents) made it up to keep us niños (kids) in line." Thiago stumbled as he eased off his barstool. "I'm out of here, amigo (friend)."

"Hey, man. I can't let you drive."

"I'm good."

"No, you're not, so give me your keys."

"I'm not giving you shit."

"I'm not going to be liable if you kill someone. I need your keys, sir." When the bartender walked from behind the counter, Thiago pulled out a switchblade. "I'm not giving you my keys, cabrón (bastard)."

The man quickly shuffled back behind the counter, then pulled out his cell phone. "I'm calling the cops."

Thiago flung a twenty-dollar bill at the man. "I'm outta here, pendejo." He snagged a bottle of tequila from behind the countertop. "And I'm taking this with me." He staggered across the parking lot over to Maria's truck and quickly sped away. About a half-mile from the bar, he turned onto a rural road to avoid the cops. Not seeing any headlights behind him, he began to relax. As he cruised down the secluded road smoking a cigar, he sang along to the song Estupido Romantico by the band Mazz.

About halfway through the song, his eyes caught a glimpse of a creature standing motionless on the side of the road. He didn't have time to make out any of the details, but it appeared to be a large bird that stood around six to seven feet tall. "What the hell?" He turned down the radio, then rubbed his face as he chuckled. "Damn. I need to lay off the tequila."

About a quarter mile further down the road, his headlights illuminated the creature again as it stood in the ditch, but this time he noticed it was a large, pale-brown owl with a face of an old woman. As she remained motionless, she seemed to be glaring right at him as he drove past her. I must be seeing shit, he thought. He quickly glanced into the rearview mirror, but only saw the red glow of his taillights on the asphalt. Then to his horror, his headlights illuminated the bottom of the creature as it flew over his truck. Its fifteen-foot wingspan made a loud swooshing sound as it disappeared into the darkness in front of him. Terrified, he slid to a stop, then quickly turned around in the ditch and began heading in the opposite direction. Panic consumed him, not only did he come to realize the story of the Lechuza wasn't just folklore, but he found himself isolated on a rural country road in the middle of the night.

To his consternation, he heard the swooshing sound again, getting louder and louder with each passing second, then the bird flew over his truck and quickly disappeared into the darkness in front of him. Realizing he made a grave mistake taking the secluded road, he recklessly spun the truck around and took off in the other direction. Frightened, he began driving around eighty miles an hour. He couldn't believe his eyes as he saw the creature in the rear-view mirror flying a few feet from the back of his truck. "No fucking way!" He shoved the gas pedal to the floorboard, bringing the truck up to a hundred and ten. As he watched the creature fade into the darkness, a slight amount of relief came over him as he chuckled, "Kiss my ass, you evil bitch!"

Suddenly, the back of his truck bounced as if a heavy load of gravel was dumped into bed. As he peered into the rear-view mirror, his cockiness changed to disbelief when he saw the witch owl crouched down in the back of the truck. Being a single cab, she was mere inches away from him, only being separated by a piece of glass, and he could clearly see the face of the witch as she glared back at him. The skin on her face appeared rough like worn leather, her dark pensive eyes were large and round, her nose took the shape of a bird's beak, sharp pointed teeth lined her mouth that stretched from ear to ear, and long black hair cascaded past her shoulders.

A wave of dread swept over Thiago as he made eye contact with the witch. "Por favor ayúdame Dios (Please help me God)!"

The witch began slowly tapping on the glass with her long claw, taunting him.

Terrified, Thiago began reciting the Canticle of Mary, or what he could remember of it. "Mi alma magnifica al Dios, Y mi espíritu se regocija en Dios mi Salvador (My soul magnifies the Lord, and my spirit rejoices in God my Savior)."

As the witch's relentless assault on the truck intensified, Thiago's apprehension grew, the thunderous pounding echoing through the cabin. He watched in fear as cracks spiderwebbed across the rear window, threatening to shatter at any moment. Determined to shake her off, he jerked the wheel forcefully, attempting to dislodge the witch from the bed of the truck. But his dismay only deepened when she climbed atop the vehicle and started pounding on the driver's side window. In a desperate panic, he slammed his foot on the brakes, bringing the truck to a screeching halt on the road.

To his surprise, the creature dislodged from the truck and swooped down to the road in front of him, gracefully landing on her feet. With fear and adrenaline coursing through his veins, he stomped the gas pedal, the engine roaring as he accelerated towards the witch. But at the last moment, with an eerie agility, she leapt into the air, vanishing into the abyss of darkness.

Panic-stricken, Thiago drove at a high rate of speed, his heart pounding in his chest, as he frantically headed toward the sanctuary of his home.

El Mexicano Loco

Consumed with terror, Thiago sped down his residential street, showing no regard for innocent bystanders that could step out from between a parked vehicle at any moment. When he approached his house, he slid sideways in the street, lost control of the truck, and crashed into the garage door.

A moment later, Maria and Diego came out of the house. When she opened the driver's door and observed Thiago was unharmed, anger swept over her. "Dammit, Thiago! Look what you've done to my truck and garage door!"

Exhibiting a frightened expression, he quickly leapt from the seat while grasping the bottle of tequila. "La vieja bruja tried to kill me!"

"What old witch?"

"Lechuza!" He frantically looked around, scanning the back of the truck first, then the top of the house and sky. "She's around here somewhere!"

An aggravated expression came over Maria as she eyed the bottle of tequila. "You're drunk."

"No, I'm not. I mean, I was, but I'm not now. An old curandero at the bar warned me

Lechuza was coming for me, but I didn't believe him."

"Lechuza is just a fairytale."

"No, she's not. I saw her with my own eyes. Lechuza is real, baby. And she's after me. Please help me."

"That's just the liquor talking."

"I'm telling you the truth, baby. I swear to Dios (God)."

Maria glanced at Diego as he stood off to the side. "Go back in the house." When he walked away, she redirected her attention back to Thiago. "You need to leave."

"Leave?"

"I don't want you staying here anymore."

Anger came over him. "Fuck that. This is my fuckin' house."

"I'm not going to debate it. I don't want you around Diego."

As she berated him, Thiago heard a swooshing sound coming from the darkness above. "Do you hear that?"

"Are you even listening to me?"

"Shhh!"

"Don't shush me."

"Do you hear that?"

"I don't hear anything."

He shoved her toward the front door. "Get your ass in the house, woman! La pinche Lechuza bruja (The fucking owl witch) is here!"

Thiago slammed the front door shut, then retrieved a double-barrel shotgun from his bedroom closet and shoved a handful of 12-gauge shells into the front pocket of his pants.

Frightened, Maria motioned to Diego. "Grab whatever you need, we're leaving."

As she quickly packed up a suitcase, Thiago peered out a window. "Where in the hell do you think you're going?"

"To my mother's house."

"You'll be safer here, so stop packing."

Maria wasn't frightened of the Lechuza. Thiago, the real monster, was the reason she wanted to leave, but she couldn't tell him that in fear he'd become aggressive. "If the old witch is after you, you know it's unsafe for me and Diego to be here. If you really want to protect us, then you know we need to leave."

He thought about it for a moment. "You're right. Once I kill that evil bitch, I'll call you."

After Maria and Diego left in an Uber, Thiago checked all the doors and windows to make sure they were locked, then he sat in a chair in the center of the living room with his shotgun in one hand and bottle of tequila in the other. Around four in the morning, Thiago startled awake when someone rang the doorbell. In a dazed stupor, he sat forward in his chair and grumbled, "Who is it!?!"

The doorbell chimed again.

"Who in the fuck is it!?!"

Someone began ringing the bell continuously at a rapid pace.

Annoyed, and still slightly buzzed, he stumbled to his feet while grasping the shotgun. "I got a fuckin' gun, asshole!"

The bell continued to ring out.

As he gathered his thoughts, he remembered the safety chain secured the door and Maria might have come back home. "Sorry, baby! I'm comin'!" The bell stopped ringing right before he swung open the door. He stomped onto the front porch with his shotgun, and when he didn't see anyone, the thought of teenagers playing doorbell ditch crossed his mind. "You pinche cabrónes (fucking bastards) better stay away from my house!" As he gazed into the darkness, he detected a scratching sound emanating from the roof. "I know you motherfuckers aren't on top of my house!" He stormed down the steps and into the front yard. When he gazed up at the roof, his heart seemed to stop when he saw the moonlight illuminating the old witch as she sat perched on the ridge. "Santo mierda (Holy shit)!" He dashed back into the house and slammed the door shut. A moment later, he began to hear a tapping sound emanating from a window. When he pulled the curtains to the side, he saw the witch staring back at him. "What the fuck do you want, you evil bitch!?!"

As she glared at him with hollow eyes, she thumped the window with her claw, cracking the glass. Thiago released the curtains and quickly fired both barrels toward the window, blowing out the glass. Gunsmoke lingered in the air as he pulled the curtain to the side with the end of his shotgun. Aggravation swept over him when he didn't see her body lying on the ground. Then to his frustration, he heard a tapping sound coming from another window. He quickly loaded the shotgun and blasted the window. A moment later, a tapping sound emanated from a third window. No sooner than he shot it out, a tapping sound echoed out from a fourth window. He started to shoot, then paused as he concluded the witch was just toying with him. "Fuck you, vieja puta (old whore)! If you try to come in here, I'll blow off your fuckin' head!"

Suddenly, the lights went out. Now surrounded by darkness, a feeling of doom swept over Thiago. Then to his consternation, he heard the back door squeak open. In a panic, he rushed into a small coat closet and hid. He could feel his heart pounding in his chest as the creaky floorboards gave away the intruder's movements. As Thiago held his breath, trying to remain as quiet as possible, the footsteps stopped right outside the closet door. His mind raced with possibilities of what could happen next. A moment of silence followed, and then he heard a faint growl. A few minutes later, the footsteps retreated, then the back door slammed shut. Thiago breathed a sigh of relief, grateful for his narrow escape, but remained in the closet for several more hours.

When he mustered up enough courage to peek out of the closet, he observed daylight shining through the windows. Notorious for their aversion to sunlight, Lechuza witches typically lurked in the cover of night. However, a flicker of concern still lingered in Thiago's mind, wondering if the witch had sought refuge in the shadows within his own house, perhaps concealed in the attic or crawl space. Determined not to take any chances, he swiftly made his way to Maria's truck. Relief came over him when the engine started, but he still wasn't sure if the truck was drivable as twisted metal from the garage door lay on the dented hood and cracked windshield. He put the shifter in reverse, and as he inched out of the rubble, the mangled sections of the garage door made a screeching sound as they scraped against the front of the truck. Thiago winced at the noise, worrying the old witch might be alerted to his escape.

As he backed into the street, the truck appeared unscathed, suggesting that it only suffered superficial damage. A few blocks away, he took a deep breath and let out a sigh of relief. A few minutes later, he pulled onto a highway, and as he drove, he couldn't shake the feeling that someone, or something, was watching him. Glancing into the rearview mirror, he saw nothing but empty roads behind him. But the sensation persisted, like a knot in his stomach. As he struggled with mixed emotions, Thiago realized he needed to break the curse. Without hesitation, he drove straight to a Catholic church.

Upon entering the house of worship, Thiago stumbled upon the priest rehearsing his upcoming sermon at the altar. "Father, I apologize for interrupting, but I need your help."

The priest set his bible aside and advanced towards him. "What can I do for you, my son?"

Thiago told him about the witch.

The priest laid his hand on Thiago's shoulder. "You are experiencing the handiwork of the devil, my son, and you must confess your sins and seek salvation."

Thiago scoffed at the religious rhetoric spewing forth from the priest's mouth. "Confess my sins? I didn't come here for that. I need your help breaking the curse."

"I'm sorry you feel that way. In our times of trouble, we must turn to Christ for help."

Thiago departed from the church feeling disheartened and desperate for answers. As he paced outside, he noticed an elderly Hispanic woman watching him intently from a nearby bench. When he approached her, she spoke in a raspy voice as she pointed at him with an old, arthritic finger. "Eres un muerto viviente."

His eyes opened wide. "What do you mean, I'm a walking dead man?"

"The old witch has returned from the grave to exact her vengeance upon you."

"Vengeance? What the hell did I do? And how do you know that she's after me? Did someone tell you that?"

"Lechuza witches only goes after the wicked. You must have done something bad to someone."

Thiago thought about the family he killed. "I haven't done anything to anyone."

"I can see it written across your face."

"You're mistaken, lady."

She shrugged her shoulders. "If you say so. But nevertheless, she wants revenge, and she won't stop until she gets it."

"How do I stop her?"

The old woman leaned closer and whispered. "You need to find her grave and destroy her body. Only then will she be at peace and leave you alone."

"How in the hell am I supposed to do that? I don't know who she is, much less where she's buried."

"There's another way."

"And?"

"If you have taken the life of another, you can use their bones to perform a cleaning ritual."

"I don't know how to do that shit."

"Then you need to seek the help of a curandero."

"Can you do it if I bring you the bones?"

"You did kill someone."

His eyes narrowed in frustration. "Can you do it or not?"

"I cannot help you."

"Then do you know of someone who can?"

"Your brother Raul can help you."

Thiago's older brother, Raul, lived in Mexico and he hadn't spoken to him since childhood. Thiago displayed a look of bewilderment as he gazed at the old woman. "How do you know about my brother?"

She rose to her feet and began hobbling away while using a cane.

"Hey! I asked you a question. How do you know about my brother?" When she didn't respond, Thiago went back to his truck, and over the next several minutes as he sat behind the wheel, he thought about his strange encounter with the old woman and reflected on his troubled past. When he was fourteen-years old, and Raul sixteen, his father killed a man during a bar fight and fled to Mexico to avoid prosecution. In the midst of this turbulent time, Raul faced his own legal woes, entangled in charges related to burglary, drug offenses, assault, and even rape. With the imminent threat of juvenile detention looming over him, Raul made the decision to flee to Mexico alongside their father, embarking on a path defined by a lifetime of criminal activities that spanned several decades.

Venganza

As Thiago sat in his truck, a mix of emotions surged within him. The notion that Raul could somehow help him break the curse left him bewildered. And how did the old woman even know about him, he wondered. No one in his family has mentioned the name Raul for many years. The weight of unanswered questions bore down on Thiago, urging him to reconnect with his estranged brother, but he didn't know where he lived in Mexico or have his contact information, and he wasn't even sure if Raul was still alive.

It was now nine o'clock in the morning, giving Thiago plenty of time before nightfall to find a way to break the curse, so he drove to a convenience store and bought a prepaid phone. With a sense of urgency, he dialed his mother's number first. He held onto a glimmer of hope, anticipating that she might know Raul's phone number. "Hey, mamá, it's T. I just wanted to let you know I'm out."

Upon hearing his voice, his mother's tone revealed a hint of concern. "Oh, that's wonderful news, but is everything okay?"

"Yeah, why do you ask?"

With a touch of surprise, she replied, "Your brother Raul called me last night and wanted your phone number. I haven't talk to him in years, so it really caught me off guard."

Thiago was taken aback, momentarily rendered silent by the unexpected revelation.

"Are you still there?"

"Yeah. It's just strange that he called you, because I was actually calling to see if you had his number."

Concern laced his mother's words as she cautioned, "I hope you're not planning on getting wrapped up in his world. You've already spent enough time in jail."

"Naw, mamá, it's not like that. I've just been thinkin' about him lately. That's all."

She sighed. "Okay. Just use your best judgment." After she gave him Raul's phone number, she asked, "How's Maria and Diego? I haven't seen them in a while."

"They're fine."

"What about you? How are you doing?"

"It's all good. I'd like to talk more and catch up, but I'm at the probation office and they just called my name."

"Okay, baby. Please call me later."

"Will do. Love ya, mamá."

"Love you too, baby."

After she hung up, Thiago's hand trembled as he slowly dialed Raul's number, his heart pounding with a mix of anticipation and anxiety. The weight of uncertainty settled upon him, for it had been a long time since he talked with his brother. The vast expanse of time and distance created an emotional chasm between them, leaving Thiago unsure of how to navigate this unexpected reconnection.

An older man with a deep voice answered. "Sí (Yeah)?"

"Is this Raul?"

"Quién es esto? (Who is this?)"

"It's your brother, Thiago."

"Hey, bro! I can't believe it's actually you." He laughed. "And you sound old as fuck, ese. I didn't recognize your voice."

"I know, man. It's been like almost forty years. And you sound old as fuck too. I thought I had dialed a nursing home."

"It's good to hear you still have your sense of humor, bro."

With the men breaking the ice, a wave of relief swept over Thiago. "Hell yeah, man. I can't believe it's been this long since we've talked. Time flew by like a motherfucker."

"It's just life, man. Sometimes shit gets in the way of the important stuff."

"How's pops doin'?"

"He married some young chica and has a different family now. I haven't talked to him in like twenty years."

"That's fucked up."

"You know how pop was. He didn't give a shit about us or mom."

"Speaking of mom, I was surprised when she said you called and wanted my number. But the crazy thing is, I called her to see if she had your number."

"Yeah, bro. I've been having these fucked up dreams about you."

"What kind of dreams?"

"Esta vieja bruja loca (This crazy old witch) was chasing you. The shit seemed real as fuck, bro, like your life is in some kind of danger."

Thiago's heart felt like it skipped a beat as he remained silent.

"Are you still there?"

"Yeah, man. Some crazy shit has been happening to me. And I'm not sure if I want to even tell you, because you'll probably think I'm loco as fuck."

"I already know, man. Someone put a hex on you, and now Lechuza is seeking venganza (revenge)."

A slight amount of relief came over him. "How do you know about that?"

"From my dreams."

"So, you know about the curse of the Lechuza?"

"Yeah, man. I've seen some strange shit down here in Mexico. Lechuza is a perra realmente malvada (real evil bitch), and folks around here take her dark magic serious as fuck. What the hell did you do to get cursed, bro?"

"I didn't do shit."

"You can tell me. I'm your brother. Hell, I've done some really fucked up shit myself, so I ain't gonna judge you."

"I was in a car accident and the people in the other vehicle died. The shit wasn't my fault. The fuckers pulled out in front of me." Thiago didn't want to admit to being wasted, so he lied. "They said I was drunk, but I only had one cerveza. I got locked up for twelve years for that bullshit, and I just got out yesterday."

"I'm not an expert at breaking curses, but I've seen enough to know we have to get their bones and perform a cleaning ritual."

"An old lady said the same thing earlier. And do you know how to do the ritual?"

"Naw, man. But I know this old curandero that does. Once we get their bones, we'll bring 'em back here to Mexico so he can do it."

"Are you planning on helping me?"

"Of course. I'm your brother. I'm packing up a bag as we speak. Are you still in Rosevine?"

"Yeah."

"Easy enough, man. I should be there first thing in the morning. Just text me your address so I can GPS that shit."

"I'm not sure where I'll be staying tonight, but when I figure it out, I'll let you know. And I'm gonna owe you big time for this."

"Naw, man. We're blood. We have to look out for each other, 'cause no one else will."

"I hear ya, bro.

"I need to wrap some shit up before I head your way, so I gotta let you go."

"Alright, man, I'll see you in the morning." Thiago hung up and then sat wondering what to do next. Knowing he needed to find a place of refuge before nightfall, he drove to an old friend's house. When he pulled up, he found his friend, Luis Torres, in the driveway working on his 1964 Chevy El Camino. Thiago wasn't sure how to approach the situation as he strolled up to him. "What's up, dog!?!"

Luis, laying on a creeper, rolled out from under the car. "Hey, man! When did you get out?"

"Yesterday."

He rose to his feet and gave Thiago a three-way handshake followed by a fist bump. "Hell, yeah, man. It's good to see you, bro."

"How have you been doin'?"

"You know, same shit different day." Luis noticed the damage to the 1978 Ford truck. "Damn, bro. What happened to Maria's truck?"

"Man, some crazy shit has been happening to me." Thiago told Luis about his encounter with the old witch, Maria going to her mother's, and that his brother was coming from Mexico in the morning to help him break the curse.

"No way, man. You must have been drunk as fuck and was just seeing shit."

Thiago motioned for Luis to follow him to the truck, then he showed him some claw marks dug into the side of the bed and on top of the cab. "Check those out. La perra malvada (The evil bitch) did this shit."

"That must have happened when you ran into the garage door."

"Naw, man. The door only fucked up the hood."

Luis scrutinized the scratches, observing they came in groups of five. "Maybe these are from some kind of wild animal, like a bear or somethin'."

"There ain't no fuckin' bears around here."

"I don't know, bro. Lechuza is just a fairytale."

"I thought the same shit until last night."

"And Raul actually believes you?"

"Yeah. That's why he's coming. And I need a place to crash until then."

"That's fine, bro. You can stay on the couch." Luis lived with his grandmother Rosa. "And Mamita Rosa will be home later, so don't say anything about la pinche Lechuza bruja (the fucking owl witch). She gets real weird about that kind of shit."

"Okay, bro, I won't."

Later that evening around seven o'clock, Rosa came through the front door as Thiago and Luis sat at the kitchen table playing cards. Displaying a frightened expression, she marched up to them using a cane and pointed at Thiago. "Debes irte ahora!"

Luis sat back in his chair. "Why does he have to leave?"

"Está maldito!"

"Cursed? Why would you say that, Mamita?"

She pointed her cane at Thiago. "The old witch is coming for you! You must leave now!"

Thiago's eyes opened wide. "How do you know that?"

"Los mirlos te siguen (The blackbirds are following you)."

"What do you mean blackbirds are following me?"

Her hands shook as she spoke in broken English. "They are the eyes of la vieja bruja during the daytime. She knows you're here and you must leave before you maldícenos (curse us too)."

Not wanting to upset his grandmother further, Luis tossed his cards on the table. "Sorry, bro. You're gonna have to find another place to stay."

"It's all good, man."

As Thiago and Luis walked outside, Rosa began rubbing oil on the front door frame, anointing her house, as she chanted scriptures. Luis followed Thiago to his truck, then leaned against the bed. "Sorry, man.

But I told you Mamita gets weird about that kind of shit."

The sound of birds squawking and chattering caught Thiago's attention, then a look of apprehension came over him when he noticed hundreds of blackbirds were circling in the air above, sitting in nearby trees, and roosting on the peak of the roof. "Oh, shit! She wasn't lying about the damn birds."

Luis glanced up at the sky for a moment, then at the roof of his house. "That's strange as fuck." A worried expression hung from his face as he glanced back at Thiago. "Damn, bro. I thought you were loco, but maybe you are cursed."

"I wasn't makin' the shit up."

"What the hell are you gonna do?"

"First, I need to find a place to get through the night, then me and Raul will take care of that evil bitch tomorrow."

"I hope it works out for you, bro."

Rosa yelled out as she stood in the doorway while shaking her finger. "Tienes que irte ahora! (You need to leave now!)"

Luis gave Thiago a quick fist bump. "Yeah, man. You better get going before Mamita has a heart attack."

As Thiago drove away, the blackbirds leapt from the trees and rooftop and began following him as the roaring sound of squawking engulfed the air.

Nursery Rhyme

Thiago wasn't sure what to do next. With the sun setting in an hour, he needed to find a place of refuge, so he decided to rent a room for the night at an older Motel 6 to save money. After making his payment, and as he walked across the parking lot toward his room, he came upon a group of young kids playing jump rope while singing a creepy nursery rhyme:

> "In the darkness of the night,
> When the moon shines bright,
> Beware of the old owl witch,
> Who flies with eerie might.
>
> Her feathers black as coal,
> Her eyes red as fire,
> She preys upon the wicked,
> With a hunger so dire.
>
> La Lechuza, La Lechuza,
> She'll snatch you up with glee,
> Take you to her dark domain,
> Where you'll never again be free.
>
> So, stay close to your home,
> Lock all the doors tight,

For the old owl witch,
Will come for you tonight."

Thiago gazed at the kids with a look of bewilderment. "Why are y'all singing that?"

They paused, standing motionless while staring back at him with deadpan expressions, then one of the kids pointed at him. "Dead man walking."

"What the hell did you say to me?"

The kids went back to jump roping.

"I asked you a question."

They ignored him as they began singing a modified version of the nursery rhyme:

"In the darkness of the night,
When the moon shines bright,
Beware of the old owl witch,
Who flies with eerie might.

Her feathers black as coal,
Her eyes red as fire,
She preys upon the wicked,
With a hunger so dire.

La Lechuza, La Lechuza,
She'll snatch Thiago up with glee,
Take him to her dark domain,
Where he'll never again be free.

Thiago got drunk and killed a family,
He better lock his doors tight,
For the old owl witch,
Will come for Thiago tonight."

Taken aback, Thiago grabbed the rope. "How in the fuck do you know my name!?!"

The kids took off running and quickly disappeared around the corner of the building. As Thiago stepped into his room, a deep unease was settling within him. The events of the past twenty hours had taken a toll on his mental state, leaving him mentally drained and anxious. With night approaching, he recognized the urgency to secure his surroundings, so he pushed his bed against the door, barricading it as best he could. A dresser was hastily positioned in front of the window, reinforcing the fragile barrier. However, as Thiago turned his attention to the smaller window in the bathroom, situated about five feet above the floor and inconveniently placed behind the toilet, he found himself at a loss. Uncertainty clouded his mind as he pondered how to effectively fortify it. Then a feeling of relief came over him when he realized he could use the bathroom door as a barricade. After he

41

popped out the hinge pins, he slid the door between the wall and toilet, locking it in place in front of the window.

As Thiago sat on the edge of the bed, his mind raced with thoughts and questions. The bizarre events of the past day still weighed heavily on him. However, the sight of his fortified room brought him a measure of solace as nightfall gradually encroached. Seeking a sense of additional security, he unzipped his duffle bag and retrieved his shotgun, placing it beside him on the bed. A tangible reassurance emanated from its presence. Then he reached for the bottle of tequila he had taken from the bar, its amber liquid serving as a companion to his troubled mind.

Thiago's eyes shot open as he jolted awake, his momentary slumber disrupted. Startled, he swiftly sat up, his reflexes guiding his hand to grasp the reassuring weight of his shotgun. As he sat dazed, he detected the faint sound of music emanating from the bathroom. Clinching his weapon, he eased across the floor toward the sound. When he approached the doorway to the bathroom, the music stopped. "Who in the fuck is in there!?!"

No one responded.

"I got a gun, asshole!"

When they didn't respond, he peaked into the bathroom. Finding no one there, his eyes then traveled to a shower curtain as it concealed the inside of the bathtub. "I know you're hiding behind the shower curtain! You better come out before I shoot your ass!" When no one responded, he used the end of the barrel to pull back the curtain. Finding it empty, a feeling of relief swept over him. But where did the music come from, he wondered. Then he remembered there was an alleyway behind the motel, prompting the notion that the sound must have come from a passing vehicle. Relieved, he took a deep breath, and as he headed out of the bathroom, a kid's voice echoed out, "dead man walking!"

He spun around and aimed his shotgun toward the back wall of the bathroom. "Who's there!?!" To his consternation, a group of kids began singing the same Lechuza nursery rhyme from the previous evening. He approached the door barricading the window and yelled, "You pequeños cabrónes (little bastards) better leave me the fuck alone!"

They continued singing.

"It's three in the morning! You better get home before I call the cops!"

Despite Thiago's threat and frustrated pleas, the children stubbornly continued singing. Their voices echoed through the motel room, filling the air with a haunting melody. In an act of desperation, Thiago pulled out his cell phone. Another layer of annoyance came over him when he observed he didn't have a signal. Then his eyes traveled to a phone sitting on a nightstand. He promptly marched over to it and dialed the office.

A man answered. "In the darkness of the night, when the moon shines bright..."

Thiago glanced at the handset for a moment as he mumbled, "What the fuck!?!" He stuck it back to his ear. "Who is this?"

The man continued to sing. "Beware of the old owl witch, who flies with eerie might..."

Thiago hung up, then dialed 911.

A female operator answered. "Her feathers black as coal, her eyes red as fire..."

"Is this 911?"

"She preys upon the wicked, with a hunger so dire...."

He slammed the headset back onto the phone's base as a wave of confusion swept over him. Then to his relief, the phone rang as the caller I.D. flashed *911 Emergency*

Services. He quicky snatched up the headset. "Hello!"

"La Lechuza, La Lechuza, she'll snatch Thiago up with glee, take him to her dark domain, where he'll never again be free."

"Who in the fuck is this!?!"

"Thiago got drunk and killed a family, he better lock his doors tight, for the old owl witch will come for Thiago tonight."

Filled with rage, he forcefully yanked the cord from the wall, severing the connection to the phone. In a burst of pent-up emotion, he flung the device across the room, its trajectory a reflection of his inner turmoil. Agitated and consumed by a deluge of racing thoughts, he began to pace back and forth, his frantic steps echoing the chaotic storm brewing within his mind.

Mentally and physically drained, he crawled into bed and covered his head with a pillow, but the relentless chorus echoing from outside pierced through his ears, making it impossible for him to fall asleep. Thirty minutes later, he scrambled out of bed as he grumbled, "Cállate unos pinche pendejos (shut up you fucking assholes)!" Anger consumed him as he stomped into the bathroom, only to be gripped by sheer terror at the sight before him. A gnarled hand, its skin wrinkled and adorned with long, menacing claws, was reaching through the window as it tried to dislodge the door from between the toilet and window.

Reacting on instinct, Thiago lunged forward, desperately grabbing hold of the barricade, and tried to push it back into place. To his horror, the old witch exhibited an unearthly strength, far beyond what he could contend with. Her growls, reminiscent of a wild animal, echoed out as she viciously clawed at the air, her aim fixed on seizing him. With fear coursing through every fiber of his being, Thiago knew he needed to act swiftly. With his mind racing and adrenaline pumping, he sprinted into the adjacent room, his eyes fixated on the shotgun resting on the bed. Grabbing the weapon with trembling hands, he felt a surge of urgency, knowing his fate would be doomed if the creature gained access to his room. With the shotgun clutched tightly, he dashed to the bathroom, but to his relief, the menacing beast had retreated leaving behind only the daunting sound of the nursery rhyme.

Thiago's taut muscles gradually loosened as he scanned the bathroom, a temporary sense of relief washing over him. The immediate threat appeared to have subsided, granting him a momentary respite from the ever-looming sense of impending doom. His gaze settled on the claw marks etched into the door, a vivid reminder of the peril he narrowly evaded. Taking a seat on the toilet, he positioned himself strategically, enabling a clear view of both the fortified barricade and the front door and window. From this vantage point, he could maintain a watchful eye over his surroundings, remaining vigilant in the face of uncertainty.

As the minutes slowly passed, Thiago endured the relentless repetition of the nursery rhyme, its haunting melody seeping into his thoughts. A whirlwind of questions spun through his mind, fueling his growing unease. *Who are these fuckin' kids? And why weren't they scared of the old witch? What is their connection to her? Are they her evil offspring?* Adding another layer of mystery to the unfolding events, he thought about the phone calls. Then a chilling realization took hold, as Thiago couldn't help but contemplate the unthinkable: Had he met his demise, only to find himself in the depths of Hell?

Cedar Creek Cemetery

Exhausted from a restless night haunted by the unrelenting repetition of the nursery rhyme, Thiago struggled to keep his heavy eyelids from closing as he perched on the toilet seat. Moments later, a sudden silence descended, abruptly halting the maddening melody. Almost synchronously, rays of gentle sunlight pierced through the windows, casting a glimmer of hope. It signaled the arrival of a new day, temporarily quelling the witch's wrath.

Thiago's gaze shifted towards his cell phone, noticing the presence of a signal. He swiftly tapped out a text message to his brother, his fingers dancing across the screen, conveying his urgent inquiry, *Had a real fucked up night, bro. Where are you at? We need to break the curse today. I don't know if I can make it through another night.*

A moment later he received a response. *30 min.*

Okay. I'm at Motel 6 on the corner of Franklin and 3rd. Room 14.

K.

About forty-five minutes later, the distinct rumble of a Harley Davidson motorcycle reached Thiago's ears. With a mixture of curiosity and cautious anticipation, he carefully slid the bed away from the front door and discreetly peered out. His gaze fell upon an older Hispanic man as he stood beside a black Harley Davidson chopper with a long front end, lowered suspension, ape-hanger handlebars, and a tall sissy bar. The man exuded an air of ruggedness, clad in faded blue jeans and a black leather jacket. A vibrant red bandana adorned his head, while shades concealed his eyes. His appearance was characterized by long salt-and-pepper hair, a thick mustache, and weathered, leather-like skin, hinting at a life shaped by experiences.

Thiago eased out the door. "Raul?"

A broad smile illuminated Raul's face as he reached out to firmly shake Thiago's hand. "Hey, bro!" The handshake quickly transitioned into an enthusiastic embrace, their bodies forming an inverted V shape, accompanied by a few friendly pats on the back. "Good to see you, man!" Raul stuck a cigarette in his mouth. "So, what the fuck happened last night?"

Thiago ushered Raul into his room, a sense of urgency in his movements. He gestured towards the claw marks scratched onto the door, evidence of the unsettling events that had unfolded. With a determined tone, he began recounting the harrowing details, explaining everything that had transpired, leaving no detail unspoken.

Raul listened attentively, his expression transitioning from curiosity to concern as he absorbed the gravity of Thiago's words. "Damn, bro. We gotta find those bones and get 'em back to Mexico."

"So, you believe me?"

"Of course. I told you I've seen some crazy shit. Do you know where the family is buried?"

"Yeah. They're in a graveyard that's just a few miles from here."

"Alright, man. Let's get this shit done."

As they drove out of the parking lot in Maria's truck, Thiago's eyes caught sight of a group of kids gathered in a nearby field. A surge of recognition mixed with frustration welled up within him. "Check that shit out. That's the fuckin' brats from last night."

Raul, glancing in the same direction, quickly noticed the mischievous grins adorning their faces as they glared back at him while standing motionless. A sense of unease prickled at the back of his neck as he observed their unsettling demeanor. "What the fuck? They are some evil lookin' motherfuckers."

"Should we go over there and talk to them?"

"Naw, man. Let's just get to the cemetery." As Thiago pulled onto a street, Raul glanced out the rear window, noticing one of the kids was ominously running his thumb across the front of his neck. The gesture sent a chilling message, symbolizing death and instilling a sense of doom within Raul. "Damn, bro. We need to get this shit done as soon as possible."

Thirty minutes later, Thiago steered the vehicle through the entrance of a cemetery, the tires rolling over the gravel path. Raul's gaze shifted towards the surroundings, his eyes scanning the weathered and intricate wrought iron fence that enclosed the sacred grounds. Stone walls sat on each side of the main entrance, and on top of them sat a large, wrought-iron arch. Below the arch hung a sign that read, *Cedar Creek Cemetery.* A sense of awe and curiosity enveloped him as he took in the scene. "How old is this place?"

"I don't know. I've never been here before. In fact, I don't even know where they're buried."

"Are you sure they're here?"

"Yeah. When I did some research on them, I found their obituary."

As Thiago navigated the eerie winding path through the cemetery, Raul's gaze was drawn to the vast expanse that unfolded before them. The sheer size of the cemetery struck him, its vastness stretching out into the distance. The tombstones, weathered and aged, marked the resting places of countless souls. The magnitude of the cemetery left Raul in awe. "How in the fuck are we gonna find them?"

"I'm not sure. I didn't expect it to be this size."

A moment later, Raul's eyes caught sight of an old man diligently hand-digging a grave in the distance. "Check out that dude. We can ask him."

Thiago, a bit hesitant, voiced his concerns. "That might make us look suspicious."

"I got an idea. Stop the truck."

When Thiago came to a stop, Raul quickly jumped out and retrieved some fresh flowers from a nearby grave. A mischievous grin played across his face as he held them up. "We'll just tell the fucker we're friends of the family."

"Good thinkin', bro." With renewed determination, Thiago pulled up alongside the man and rolled down his window. "Excuse me, sir!"

The man, dressed in dirt-stained blue jeans, a red flannel shirt, and distressed work boots, turned his attention towards the truck. Atop his head sat a battered cowboy hat, its brim weather-beaten and frayed, bearing witness to the countless hours spent under the sun's scorching rays. Long strands of grey hair flowed down his shoulders, a testament to a life enriched with wisdom and experience. The creases and lines etched on his face revealed the passage of time, while his tan, weathered skin spoke volumes about his toil in the unforgiving elements. With a calm and rugged presence, the old man approached the truck, his eyes filled with curiosity. "How can I help you?"

"We're lookin' for the Dawson family. We're close friends of theirs. They were buried here about twelve years ago."

The old man scratched his chin as he thought. "Oh, yeah. John and Martha, and their two kids, Ethan and Chloe." He paused for a moment, his gaze sweeping across the sprawling expanse of the cemetery. With a knowing nod, he extended his hand and pointed toward a specific direction, his voice filled with a hint of wisdom. "Spring Grove Lane, section twelve, lot four, spaces seven through ten."

Thiago, feeling overwhelmed by the sheer size of the cemetery, gazed at the old man with confusion etched on his face. "And where exactly is that?"

From his shirt pocket, the man produced a stack of neatly folded papers. Carefully selecting one from the group, he unfolded it, revealing a detailed map of the cemetery. With a steady hand, he retrieved a pencil from his pocket and circled a specific area on the paper, marking their intended destination before handing it to Thiago. "It's a shame what happened to that family," the old man remarked, his voice filled with a tinge of sorrow.

Thiago's heart sank as he heard those words, for he knew he was the reason the family was there. However, contrary to expectations, remorse did not fill his heart. Instead, a bitter undertone coursed through him, a direct result of the twelve long years he spent behind bars. The weight of the past and the hardships endured during his time of confinement had left an indelible mark, fueling a sense of resentment that overshadowed any guilt he might have felt. Thiago scrutinized the map. "Thanks. This makes it a lot easier."

"I'm Ben Hamilton, the gravedigger. I'm here all day, every day, so if you need anything else, don't hesitate to ask."

"Will do." As Thiago pulled away, he handed the map to Raul. "Hell yeah, man. That was easy as fuck."

While Thiago drove, Raul used the map to guide them along the winding paths of the cemetery. When they finally reached their destination, they parked the truck and stepped out, making their way toward the graves that awaited them. As Thiago stood before the tombstones, a surreal and haunting sensation washed over him. His gaze fixed upon the names engraved into the cold granite: John, Martha, Ethan, and Chloe. Raul took notice of the ages etched beside their names—Ethan at thirteen, Chloe at eight. Sensing his brother's distress, he spoke with an empathetic tone, attempting to provide solace. "Accidents happen, bro. You didn't do the shit on purpose."

Reluctant to bear the full burden of guilt, especially since he knew the accident was ultimately his fault, Thiago nodded, his expression guarded. "Yeah, man," he
56

replied, his voice tinged with bitterness. "I just wish they hadn't pulled out in front of me. It cost me twelve years of my life." His words revealed the deep-seated resentment he harbored, the belief that circumstances beyond his control had unjustly robbed him of precious years. The pain of the past lingered, its grip on his heart unyielding, refusing to release him from its torment.

Raul placed the flowers next to Chloe's tombstone. "Now that we know where they're buried at, we need to figure out how we're gonna dig 'em up. And with that old man hanging around, we'll have to come back tonight."

A look of concern came over Thiago. "Tonight? That's when that evil bitch will be out."

"Don't sweat it, bro. I brought some protection."

"What kind of protection?"

"Twelve-gauge shotgun rounds loaded with a mixture of salt, spices, and coffin nails."

"Will that shit work?"

"According to Santiago it will. He's the one who gave them to me."

"Who in the fuck is Santiago?"

"The old curandero who lives in my town. He's also the one who's gonna perform the cleaning ritual."

Thiago redirected his focus back to the graves. "I didn't think this shit through. How in the hell are we gonna dig up four graves?"

Raul nodded toward a backhoe parked under a large oak tree. "Check out that backhoe. I saw it earlier when we first got here. We can use that."

"I doubt it even works."

Raul noticed the machine appeared to be just a few years old, and on the side was an orange decal that read, *Mahan Rentals.* "It's a rental, so I bet it does."

"Then why isn't that old man using it?"

"I don't fuckin' know. Maybe his ass likes diggin' graves by hand." He thought for a moment. "You know what. Some contractors probably rented it."

Thiago scanned the cemetery. "I don't see any work going on."

"Maybe they haven't started yet." He nodded. "Let's go check it out."

Thiago and Raul nonchalantly strolled over to the backhoe. Finding the key in the ignition, Raul reached for it, but a worried expression came over Thiago. "Hold up, bro. That old man might hear it."

"Fuck him." Raul turned the key, and when the engine fired up, he quickly shut it off. "Hell yeah, bro! We're gonna use this shit." He held up the map. "And now that we know where the family is at, we'll be in and out in no time."

A huge amount of anxiety drained from Thiago. "This is gonna be easier than I thought."

When they got back in the truck, Raul studied the map for a moment, then pointed. "Go that way."

"But the gate is the other direction."

"I know, but I want to see if there is a back entrance."

As they drove along the backside of the cemetery, Raul observed the wrought iron fence ran around the entire perimeter, and he could see the surrounding property was heavily wooded. "Damn. Looks like we're gonna have to come in from the front."

"We could rent one of those gas-powered cut-off saws and cut the fence."

Raul pulled out his phone and opened Google Maps. "Naw, man. It's too wooded. I'm not walkin' through that shit."

"We could bring some machetes and cut a path."

"Fuck that. We'll just sneak in from the front."

As they drove through the double gates at the front entrance, Raul observed a sign that read, *No Access to Cemetery Between 10 PM and 6 AM. Trespassers Will Be Prosecuted.* "This place is locked up after ten, so we'll come back around one AM." He ogled the chain and pad lock dangling from one of the gates. "We need to bring some bolt cutters so we can drive right up to the graves."

"I already have a pair under the seat."

"Hell yeah, bro. We'll be in and out of here in a jiffy."

"Sounds good. Let's go find a bar. I need a drink."

"Now you're talkin'."

Doomed

Around midnight back at the motel, Raul awoke Thiago. "Hey, bro. It's time to go."

Thiago sat forward in a chair and rubbed his eyes. "I didn't mean to fall asleep." When he glimpsed the time on his cell phone, observing it was nighttime, panic swept over him. "Oh, shit! Lechuza is out!" He rushed to the bathroom and scrutinized the door still wedged between the toilet and window.

Raul ambled up behind him. "It's all good, man. It's been quiet."

"Really?"

"Yeah."

"What about those fuckin' kids?"

"Not a peep from them either."

"Do you think it's over? Maybe we don't have to dig up those graves."

Before Raul could respond, a voice echoed from the depths of the alleyway, piercing the night with its petrifying tone. "Dead men walking!" The words hung in the air, a haunting proclamation that sent shivers down Thiago's spine.

Raul chuckled, his laughter filled with a mix of amusement and defiance. "You just got your answer, bro."

Thiago's brow furrowed in confusion. "Why are you laughing? The little fucker said men, so that includes you too."

A mischievous glint sparkled in Raul's eyes as he raised Thiago's shotgun, its metallic weight providing a semblance of security. "I'm not sweating it. I've got this shit loaded with the coffin nails." With a swift motion, he revealed two necklaces adorned with rows of garlic bulbs, their pungent scent filling the air. "And I've got these." He stuck one around his own neck, then tossed the other one to Thiago.

As Thiago scrutinized the crude necklace, his fingers examined the twine that held the protective bulbs together. "What the hell is this?"

"Santiago made these for us to ward off evil spirits. That's why that old bitch hasn't come around."

"I thought this shit only worked for vampires."

"You watch too much TV, bro."

"And maybe she's just waiting for us to leave the room."

"Naw, man. Santiago is a well-known curandero. He's like a hundred-years old and his juju is strong. With these garlic talismans and the coffin nails, that old bitch won't dare to come near us."

Thiago felt a small surge of relief wash over him, hope glimmering in his eyes. "I hope you're right, man."

Raul confidently pushed the bed away from the front door and stepped outside, his arms outstretched as if embracing the night. The moonlight cast shadows across his face as he slowly rotated, firmly clutching the shotgun. See, it's all good, man."

Thiago hesitantly leaned against the doorway, his gaze fixated on the dark expanse above. "You're crazy, bro."

Raul's eyes twinkled with a blend of mischief and resolve. "Don't be scared. That bitch ain't comin' near us as long as we have Santiago's magic with us."

Together, they stood in the night, armed with the symbols of protection and defiance. The shotgun held the promise of earthly defense, while the garlic necklaces embodied the ancient wisdom passed down through generations, shielding them by the powerful magic of Santiago's curative touch.

Raul opened the passenger's side of Maria's truck. "Let's get this shit done, bro."

Thiago examined the roof of the motel for a moment, then scrutinized the sky above.

When he didn't spot the old witch, he took a deep breath. "Okay, man." He climbed into the driver's seat. "I'm glad you came. I wouldn't have been able to do this on my own."

"I'm your brother. I'll always be here for you."

When they arrived at Cedar Creek Cemetery, Raul jumped out with a pair of bolt cutters. After messing with the gates for a few minutes, he climbed back into the truck. "The fuckin' chain is too big to cut, and the padlock is one of those shrouded types."

"Seriously?"

"Fuck yeah."

"Didn't you notice that earlier?"

"It's a different chain and lock. But it has enough slack where we can slip between the gates, but we're not gonna be able to take the truck."

"Do you think that old man saw us messin' with the backhoe and swapped them out?"

"I don't think so. If he wanted to keep us out, he would have made sure to keep the gates tight." Raul pointed to a group of trees on the other side of the road. "Let's hide the truck behind that brush. We'll go on foot from here."

"I'm not walking through that damn cemetery, especially at night."

"We don't have a choice."

"I can run through the gates."

"Naw, man. They're heavy duty. And it will make too much noise."

After maneuvering the truck into a concealed spot behind a cluster of trees, Thiago and Raul quickly disembarked and retrieved their gear. Flashlights in hand, they sprinted back to the entrance of the cemetery, their footsteps echoing through the stillness of the night. Thiago gripped the cold metal of a sturdy tire iron, its weight providing a sense of reassurance in his hands. His eyes scanned the surroundings, ready to confront any lurking threat that dared to cross their path.

Raul, armed with the trusty shotgun, moved beside Thiago with purposeful strides. The weapon embodied a tangible symbol of protection, its presence empowering him with a heightened sense of security. With every beat of his heart, he channeled a primal energy, prepared to defend against whatever malevolent forces they might encounter within the depths of the cemetery.

As they slipped through the gates, a unsettling sensation washed over Thiago, causing his skin to prickle with unease. The stark contrast between the moonlit world outside the cemetery walls and the enigmatic darkness within intensified the eerie atmosphere. Outside the confines of the cemetery, the moon's ethereal glow painted a serene picture, casting a soft radiance upon the surroundings. However, as they ventured deeper into the graveyard, the moonlight struggled to penetrate the thick canopy of overgrown trees, leaving the interior shrouded in an impenetrable gloom. A feeling of dread washed over Thiago. "This place is creepy as fuck. Maybe we should rethink this."

"Yeah, it does have a fucked-up vibe. But we'll be in and out of here in no time, so, let's get this shit done."

A pervasive sense of mystery hung in the air, gripping their senses and heightening their awareness. The temperature dropped noticeably, creating an unsettling chill that seemed to seep into their very bones. Each breath they took seemed to fog in front of them, a visible testament to the frigid presence that enveloped the cemetery. The scent of death, subtle yet unmistakable, mingled with the nocturnal breeze, carrying with it a somber reminder of the finality of life.

It lingered in the air, a haunting perfume that whispered of souls long departed.

The night seemed to possess an uncanny energy within the cemetery's confines, an energy that raised the hairs on the back of their necks. Each step they took carried a weight of trepidation, their eyes scanning the surroundings for any sign of movement or the faintest glimmer of a ghostly presence. The rustling of leaves, occasional creak of old trees, or the distant hoot of an owl sent shivers down their spines, amplifying the unnerving atmosphere that enveloped them. Each step they took felt like an intrusion into the realm of the deceased, as if the spirits watched their every move with a mixture of curiosity and caution.

Thiago couldn't escape the overwhelming sense of trespassing in this hallowed realm, where the boundary between the world of the living and the realm of the departed appeared to blur. Within these sacred grounds, the weight of forgotten stories and untold secrets hung heavy in the air, as if the very fabric of time whispered ancient mysteries that yearned to be unraveled. It was a place where the living and the dead converged, their essence intertwining in an ethereal dance of existence. A shiver coursed through Thiago's body, a primal instinct urging him to retreat from the enigmatic embrace of the graveyard. "I'm not sure about this, man. Maybe we should turn back. Something feels wrong."

Raul, equally affected by the negative energy that encompassed the cemetery, shared Thiago's unease. Every fiber of his being longed to escape this place of spectral whispers and lingering despair. However, a flicker of determination burned in his eyes as he recognized the grim reality they faced. The bones of the family were the key to breaking the curse that plagued his brother. "We don't have a choice. If we're going to break the curse, we have to get the bones."

Thiago swallowed hard, feeling the weight of their predicament pressing down upon him. He nodded, acknowledging the gravity of their situation. "I know."

"Just man up and let's get this done."

With a mix of trepidation and resolve, they continued to move through the eerie expanse of the dark, creepy cemetery, their footsteps muffled by the soft crunch of fallen leaves and overgrown grass. The moon's feeble light struggled to penetrate the thick canopy of gnarled trees, casting eerie shadows that danced and flickered in the night breeze.

The tombstones, weathered and worn, loomed ominously in the dim light, standing as silent sentinels of the deceased.

Their senses heightened, Thiago and Raul couldn't help but feel a tingling sensation crawl up their spines, a primal instinct warning them of unseen dangers lurking in the darkness. The air itself seemed to hold a palpable sense of foreboding, as if the spirits of the departed whispered warnings that only they could hear. As they ventured deeper into the labyrinth of tombstones, the darkness seemed to close in around them, the veil between the living and the dead growing ever thinner. The distant glow of the moon eventually became so obscured by the dense canopy overhead, it left them to navigate only by the faint glow of their flashlights, casting eerie shadows that danced and played tricks on their minds.

The atmosphere held an otherworldly quality, a mixture of anticipation and dread that seemed to saturate the air. They moved cautiously, their every breath a testament to the tension that gripped them. The flickering shadows and the silence of the graveyard created a sense of being watched, as if unseen eyes observed their every move.

Thiago and Raul pressed forward, their nerves on edge, knowing that within the dark and eerie cemetery, the unknown awaited them, ready to reveal its secrets or unleash its malevolence at any given moment. Suddenly, a raven perched in a nearby tree cried out, "DOOOOMED!"

Thiago paused in his tracks. "Did you hear that shit!?!"

"Yeah, it's just a fuckin' bird."

"It said, "doomed"."

"That's just your mind playing tricks on you."

"Seriously, bro. The fuckin' thing yelled out "doomed"."

Before Raul could respond, the raven leaped from a nearby branch, its majestic wings carrying it into the shrouded depths of the night. As it vanished into the darkness while repeating the word "doooomed", the unsettling echo reverberated through the air, filling the atmosphere with a sinister presence.

Thiago and Raul exchanged wary glances, their senses heightened by the unnerving encounter. "I told you it said "doomed"."

The message conveyed by the raven's departure and the haunting echo weighed heavily on Raul, adding an extra layer of foreboding to their already perilous journey. "That's probably just that evil bitch fuckin' with us. She knows why we're here and doesn't want us to get the bones."

Thiago clutched the garlic hanging from around his neck. "I thought this shit was supposed to keep her away."

"It is. That's why she's not showing herself and just using trickery to scare us."

They tightened their grips on their weapons, finding solace in the presence of each other as they pressed forward, ready to face the unknown and challenge the sinister forces that awaited them in the depths of the night.

A Night of Horror

As Raul made his way through the darkness, he realized that Thiago was no longer trailing behind him. With concern etched into his face, he swung his flashlight around, searching for his brother's whereabouts in the shadows. Finally, his beam of light fell upon Thiago, standing motionless beside a bone-white tree devoid of any leaves. "What the hell are you doing? We got to keep goin'."

Thiago seemed unfazed by Raul's question, his attention fixated on the bizarre tree before him. Ignoring his brother's inquiry, he continued to stare intently at the eerie sight.

Raul closed the distance between them, his steps quickened by a growing sense of concern. The beam of his flashlight illuminated his brother's face, revealing furrowed brows and a troubled expression. "What's going on, bro?"

Thiago directed his flashlight towards the tree, revealing a disturbing revelation. As he peeled away the white bark, an unsettling sight unfolded before their eyes. Crimson droplets of blood emerged from within the tree, trickling out and staining the ground below as the air grew heavy with an ominous

73

presence. Thiago's heart pounded in his chest as he absorbed the gravity of their situation. The sight before them was an undeniable testament to the malevolence that permeated their surroundings.

Unnerved yet determined, Raul motioned with his flashlight. "We got to keep going."

"I don't know, man. Between the raven and now this tree, maybe we need to turn back."

"If we don't get those bones tonight, we might not have another chance."

"We can come back during the daytime."

"Not with that old man around."

"I think we're making a big mistake. We need to heed the warnings."

"Like I said, that evil bitch is just using trickery to scare us away. If something bad was going to happen to us, it would already have, so stop worrying, bro."

Suddenly, Thiago's senses heightened as he caught a faint noise, barely audible amidst the eerie silence. His head turned, searching for confirmation from his brother. "Do you hear that?"

Raul strained his ears, his expression transforming into one of alertness. "Yeah, man. Sounds like someone is playing a radio or something."

"Who in the fuck would be out here this time of night?"

"I don't know, but we need to see who it is."

"Fuck that."

"If someone is out here, we can't use the backhoe because they will hear it and call the cops."

"Shit. You're right. I didn't think of that."

"Besides, it could just be a radio the old man left on."

As they crept through the darkness with their flashlights off, slowly heading toward the sound, they came upon a group of kids playing jump rope. An old oil-burning lantern hung from a tree limb above them, casting their eerie shadows on the ground. Thiago crouched behind a tombstone as he watched in disbelief. "I recognize some of those kids. They're the same ones from back at the motel. But I don't recognize the other two, the ones holding the rope."

"What the hell are they doing out here at this time of night?"

"I don't know, man, but it's creepy as fuck."

As Raul listened closely, he could hear them singing the Lechuza nursery rhyme:

"La Lechuza, La Lechuza,
She'll snatch Thiago and Raul up with glee,
Take them to her dark domain,
Where they'll never again be free.

Thiago got drunk and killed a family,
Raul sold dope and lived a life of crime,
La Lechuza is coming for them tonight,
So, they better run and hide."

Raul eyed Thiago with a look of consternation. "How in the fuck do they know my name?"

"Because they're fuckin' evil."

"I'm gonna move in closer to get a better look."

"Naw, man. We need to get the fuck out of here."

"You can hang back, but I'm gettin' closer to see what the hell is going on."

Reluctantly, Thiago trailed behind his brother as they made their way through the darkness, stopping when they were around thirty feet away from the children. Seeking refuge behind a large tombstone, Thiago and

Raul positioned themselves discreetly, their eyes fixed upon the group of children. Dread gripped their hearts as they observed the ghastly appearance of the young ones before them. The children's flesh was decayed, their eyes vacant and hollow, while their tattered and dirt-stained clothing added to the haunting visage they presented.

In a horrifying scene, a teenage boy and a young girl twirled what initially appeared to be a thick rope in their hands. However, as Thiago focused his gaze, a surge of revulsion shot through him. It wasn't a rope they spun but the girl's intestine, gruesomely protruding from her rear end. With every rotation, the organ swung in a morbid dance, the sight chilling the brothers to their core.

A mixture of shock and repulsion overwhelmed Thiago as he witnessed this grotesque spectacle. The boundaries of their reality seemed to blur in the face of such unimaginable horror. The children's disturbing play painted a vivid picture of the twisted darkness that enveloped his nightmarish realm. "Are you seeing this? They're some kind of zombies or something."

"There are no such thing as zombies. This is just more of that bitch's trickery."

As Thiago's eyes adjusted to the dark, a feeling of dread came over him when he recognized the boy and girl. "Oh, my god! It's the kids from the accident."

"What are you talkin' about?"

"The boy and girl slinging the intestine. It's Ethan and Chloe. You know, the kids from the car wreck. The Dawson kids."

"Bullshit. That's impossible."

"I'm not fuckin' with you, bro. It's them."

"Your eyes are just playin' tricks on you."

In a frightening turn of events, the children suddenly halted their eerie game. Slowly and deliberately, they pivoted as one, fixing their vacant gazes directly upon Thiago and Raul. A wave of trepidation crashed over Thiago, causing a shiver to course through him. The unnerving stillness of the children, coupled with their unsettling appearances, intensified the sense of foreboding that had settled within him. Each passing moment further solidified the realization that they were facing something far more sinister and otherworldly than they could have ever anticipated. "Oh, fuck! They know we're here."

Raul, attempting to maintain a semblance of calm, refuted Thiago's fear. "There's no way. We're hidden in the dark."

However, their hopes of remaining unnoticed were shattered when the smallest child, a haunting figure with missing eyes, decaying skin, and seated on the ground due to the absence of legs, pointed a bony finger towards the brothers. In a horrifying, ear-piercing shriek, the child wailed out the words that froze their blood. "Dead men walking!"

Horror seized Thiago and Raul as the children began to move towards them, their twisted and disfigured forms sending chills down their spines. Some of the children were surprisingly fast, defying their grotesque appearances, while others struggled with their twisted and deformed limbs, moving at a slower pace. Chloe's intestines dragged behind her as she staggered forward on unsteady legs, while the child with no legs used his arms to crawl along the ground.

The scene unfolded like a nightmare, each child's twisted and deformed body intensifying the horror that gripped Thiago and Raul. It was a tableau of the unimaginable, a visceral manifestation of their deepest fears brought to life.

As the children closed in, a chilling realization washed over the brothers. These were not innocent children, but twisted entities that defied reason and comprehension. Raul leaped to his feet, his voice quivering with panic. "Run!"

Thiago followed behind his brother as they chaotically ran through the graveyard, their desperate escape hampered by the darkness that enveloped their surroundings. With each frantic step, they collided with tombstones, the impact jarring their bodies, and stumbled over the uneven ground and treacherous roots that lurked beneath the leaves.

Their horror escalated as the growls of the children echoed through the night, resembling feral creatures lurking in the depths of the darkness, taunting them with their haunting presence. Fear surged through their veins, propelling them forward with a desperate determination to escape the clutches of these monstrous entities.

As their legs grew heavier and their breaths became deep and labored, Thiago and Raul stumbled upon an old stone structure nestled in a secluded corner of the cemetery. Driven by sheer terror, Raul lunged towards the steel door, his waning strength bolstered by the urgency of the situation. With every ounce of energy he could muster, he clasped the handle and exerted a final burst of effort. In that crucial moment, a profound sense of relief flooded over him as the door yielded to his touch, swinging open to reveal a flicker of hope amidst the encroaching evilness. Without a moment's hesitation, they darted inside, seeking temporary refuge from their pursuers. The heavy steel door creaked shut behind them, sealing them in the suffocating darkness of the tomb.

Gasping for breath, Thiago and Raul pressed themselves against the door as the eerie silence within the building was disrupted only by their frantic whispers and the muffled sounds of the children's growls echoing from outside. Breathing a sigh of relief, Thiago and Raul took a moment to collect themselves. They knew they had narrowly escaped a malevolent force, but they also realized that their ordeal was far from over.

Raul sank to the ground with his shotgun in hand, keeping his back against the door. "Holy fuck, dude! That was close."

Exhausted, Thiago collapsed beside him. "What the hell are those things?"

"I don't know, man. But you were right. We should have never come here."

"Don't beat yourself up, bro. Neither one of us could have known this would happen."

Suddenly, an eerie silence fell upon the building, shattering the previous whispers and growls that had filled the air. Thiago and Raul exchanged cautious glances, their senses heightened as they strained to listen for any new sounds or movements. The absence of the haunting whispers and feral growls raised a sense of apprehension within them. It was as if the very presence that had pursued them had momentarily retreated, lurking in the shadows with unknown intentions.

Thiago tightened his grip on his tire iron, his knuckles turning white. "Do you think they're gone?"

Raul shook his head slowly, his voice barely a whisper. "I'm not sure, but we can't let our guard down. They could be waiting for us to come out."

Their surroundings remained enveloped in an unsettling stillness, amplifying the tension that hung in the air. Each passing second felt like an eternity, fueling their growing unease. "Now what are we gonna do?"

Raul lit a cigarette, then took a long drag as he kept his back against the door. "We'll just hang out here until morning. Once the sun comes out, they should be gone."

Thiago swept his flashlight across the interior of the building, revealing a sight that filled him with both curiosity and unease. The structure appeared to be very old, as the stone walls bore the signs of time with brown and green patina. A thin film of dust blanketed every surface, and intricate spiderwebs adorned the corners and crevices, creating a haunting ambiance. In the center of the structure stood several large concrete vaults, and along the back, rows upon rows of square ornamental panels adorned the wall. "What is this place?"

Raul took a moment and scrutinized the surroundings. "It's an old mausoleum."

Thiago's eyes then caught sight of oil-burning lanterns suspended from the walls. "I wonder if those lamps work."

Raul tossed him his Zippo lighter. "See if you can get them to light."

Thiago meticulously lit each lantern, their gentle glow cascading through the small burial chamber, bringing a sense of solace and comfort. The warm illumination provided a temporary sanctuary from the terrors that lurked outside. With a newfound sense of tranquility, Thiago shifted his attention toward the bronze panels. With a mixture of curiosity and reverence, his fingers gently traced the engraved names and dates. "What are these plaques for? They have people's names and dates written on them."

"They're crypts."

Thiago's confusion deepened, a perplexed expression on his face. "So, there are dead bodies inside the wall?"

"Yeah, but they're most likely entombed inside caskets."

His curiosity grew as he read some of the engravings on the panels. "Damn. Some of these go all the way back to the early 1800s."

"Yeah, man. This place is old as fuck."

Surrounded by the echoes of the past, Thiago continued reading the names and dates on the panels. Each one creating curiosity as to who the person was and how they might have died. Then to his horror, his heart skipped a beat when his own name emerged before him. His breath caught in his throat, and a horrifying sensation washed over him. With trembling hands, he pointed out the plaque to Raul, his voice laced with disbelief and fear. "Oh shit! Someone put my name on here." Then he noticed Raul's name was engraved on the adjacent plaque. "And your name is on this one."

"Bullshit."

"I'm serous, bro."

"It's probably just a coincidence. Thiago and Raul are common names."

"It's not just our first names. It's our full names; Thiago Angel Martinez, and Raul Emiliano Martinez. Even our birthdates are correct. And the date of death is today's date."

Raul stumbled to his feet and quickly approached his plaque. At first, a feeling of dread came over him as he read his name, followed by anger. "That old bitch must have done this to fuck with us."

An unsettling silence filled the mausoleum, amplifying the weight of the ominous message in the form of their names immortalized among the deceased. Dread settled within them, mingling with a surge of anger and confusion. What sinister force was behind this twisted revelation? Was it the handiwork of the old witch, or from some other malevolent being that they haven't even encountered yet? The answers remained elusive, lost within the shadows of the mausoleum.

As fear and uncertainty gripped the brothers, they couldn't escape the sinking feeling that they had stumbled into something far beyond their comprehension. The mausoleum, once a place of solace and refuge, now became a haunting reminder of the evil presence that lurked outside in the darkness.

Suddenly, an eerie scratching sound emanated from the other side of the bronze plaque engraved with Thiago's name. "What the fuck!?! Do you hear that?"

Raul leaned closer, pressing his ear against the metallic surface. "Yeah. It's probably just a rat."

In a spine-chilling twist, the screws securing the four corners of Raul's plaque began to loosen, slowly turning as if an invisible force was at work. Dread washed over Thiago, causing him to stumble backwards. "Are you seeing this!?! Something's trying to get out of your tomb!"

Raul gazed at the loosening screws, his expression a blend of disbelief and confusion. "What the hell? How is that possible? And that's not my fuckin' my tomb."

Then, to their utter horror, the plaque detached from the wall, crashing to the floor with a resounding thud. Thiago, gripped by fear, instinctively raised his flashlight, casting its beam into the vacant depths of the vault. As he realized it was empty, a wave of relief washed over him, though a trace of unease still lingered. He gasped, his voice tinged with a mixture of relief and lingering apprehension. "There's nothing in there."

"That doesn't make any sense. Then how in the fuck did those screws back out?"

"I don't know, man."

Suddenly, a cool breeze enveloped Raul, raising the hairs on the back of his neck, while an eerie whisper seemed to resonate within him, beckoning him toward his tomb. "Oh, shit! Did you hear that?"

"Hear what?"

"Something wants me to get inside that vault."

"What the hell are you talking about, bro?"

"Something told me to get inside my vault, like it wants to entomb me in there."

"I didn't hear anything. Your mind must be playing tricks on you."

In that very moment, a white substance splattered onto Thiago's shoulder, causing him to react instinctively by rubbing it between his fingers. As the material felt oddly familiar, like bird shit, his face twisted in confusion. "What the hell?" he muttered, his voice tinged with bewilderment. When he directed his gaze toward the ceiling, his eyes widened in sheer terror at the sight of the old witch perched in the rafters. "Oh my God! It's fuckin' Lechuza!"

Raul, unable to comprehend what he was witnessing, stared in horror at the haunting figure. It was his first encounter with her. The witch's body took the shape of a large owl, her weathered face bore the texture of worn leather, her dark, penetrating eyes were large and round, her nose resembled a bird's beak, and sharp, pointed teeth lined her mouth, stretching from ear to ear. Long black hair cascaded down her shoulders, completing the bone-chilling image.

Both men stood frozen in fear as the witch gracefully descended from the rafters, landing on her feet with an unnerving poise. With a bony finger tipped with a long, sharp claw, she pointed directly at Raul before gesturing toward the open vault, beckoning him forth with a haunting invitation. Raul raised his shotgun. "No way you fuckin' bitch! I'm not gettin' in there!" Without hesitation, he pulled both triggers simultaneously, unleashing the thunderous blast of the twelve-gauge rounds. The devastating impact propelled the witch backward, the coffin nails tearing into her body and face. She collided forcefully with the wall before collapsing onto the floor. To their disbelief, she rose to her feet, then in an act of defiance, pulled one of the coffin nails from her face, a wicked grin spreading across her features. With an eerie gleam in her eyes, she began licking off the spices from the nail, taunting them.

Without uttering a word, both men darted out the door and sprinted into the encompassing darkness. Their hearts pounded in their chests as they pushed themselves to the limit, their bodies fueled by adrenaline. But as their energy waned, they eventually reached their breaking point, gasping for air and struggling to continue. Raul, his hands on his knees, pleaded for a brief respite. "Hold up, bro. I need to catch my breath."

Thiago, breathing heavily, vented his frustration. "Dude! I thought Santiago knew what the fuck he was doing. Those coffin nails didn't do shit." He angrily ripped the talisman from around his neck and threw it to the ground. "Santiago is a fuckin' idiot, and now we're stuck in this cemetery with that evil bitch."

Raul, at a loss for words, shook his head. "I don't know what to think."

"We need to find the exit and get the fuck out of here."

"I know, man. Let me catch my breath first."

Suddenly, a nerve-racking voice pierced through the darkness, echoing around them. "Dead men walking!"

Thiago grasped Raul's shoulder as he urgently pulled him forward. "We have to get the fuck out of here now!"

Completely drained and with heavy footsteps, the two men began walking briskly, pushing themselves forward even in their state of exhaustion. Relief came over Thiago when he saw the entrance. "There it is! Let's get the fuck out of here!"

With a surge of adrenaline, the men sprinted to the entrance. Raul tried to slip between the gates, but quickly realized someone repositioned the padlock, tightening the chain. "Oh, fuck! I can't get through."

Breathing heavily, Thiago shined his light on the gates where they came together. "What do you mean? We were able to get through it earlier."

"I know. But someone redid the chain, now it's too tight."

A solemn expression came over Thiago. "This place is cursed, and it's not going to let us leave." Anger swept through him. "We've been lured here, and now we're doomed."

Retribution

Thiago and Raul exchanged anxious glances, their minds racing with fear and uncertainty. Before they could contemplate their next move, the old witch descended from the ominous night sky, landing gracefully atop the towering gates. Their hearts pounding, the two men turned on their heels and sprinted back into the depths of the cemetery, desperate to escape the clutches of the menacing beast.

As the men moved forward, an ominous presence loomed above them. High above the trees, the witch glided with an eerie grace. The swooshing sound of her wings echoed through the night, piercing the darkness like the harbinger of death. The haunting sound made their blood curdle, intensifying their fear and driving them to hasten their pace. Each whoosh of her wings served as a chilling reminder that the witch was close behind, relentless in her pursuit.

Their frantic escape was soon hindered by an unexpected sight—standing in their path was one of the children, motionless and expressionless. Thiago and Raul abruptly changed their course, veering away from the child and darting in a different direction. But as they continued to run, their path was repeatedly altered by the appearance of more children, strategically positioned to divert their direction. It became clear that the children were guiding them along a predetermined route, their intentions veiled in mystery.

The eerie presence of the children, coupled with the relentless pursuit of the witch, heightened the men's terror. They pressed on, their footsteps echoing through the silent graveyard, navigating the maze-like paths that seemed to twist and turn at the whims of their malevolent guides. Their minds raced with questions. Who were these children, and what role did they play in this supernatural nightmare? Were they allies or pawns in a twisted game orchestrated by the witch? Thiago and Raul had no choice but to follow their cryptic guidance, hoping they could find a way out of the macabre labyrinth they found themselves trapped in.

Their hearts sank as they stumbled upon a horrifying sight. A row of children stood before them, their innocent faces twisted into sinister expressions. The sight alone was enough to send shivers down their spines, but what lay between the children and the two men was even more disturbing.

Numerous oil-burning lanterns hung from the branches of the surrounding trees, and the graves of the Dawson family, four in total, stretched out in front of them. Each grave had been dug up, John's and Martha's caskets still closed, but Ethan's and Chloe's caskets lay open, exposing their empty interiors. The realization struck them like a punch to the gut—something unholy had transpired here, something that defied reason and sanity.

Thiago and Raul exchanged bewildered glances, their minds racing to comprehend the horrifying scene before them. The children remained unnervingly silent, their eyes fixed on the men, their presence both menacing and enigmatic. It was as if they were mere witnesses to the unfolding horror, their purpose and allegiance unknown. The two men braced themselves for what lay ahead, summoning their courage to face the sinister forces at play. The enigmatic children, the open graves, and the ominous presence of the witch above—all were pieces of a puzzle that demanded solving, a web of mysteries they had no choice but to untangle.

Before Thiago and Raul could react, around a hundred children emerged from the shadows holding lanterns, forming a large encircling ring around them, preventing them from escaping. Forty feet in diameter, the circle tightened its grip, like a macabre performance unfolding before their very eyes. The children remained eerily silent, their gazes fixated on Thiago and Raul with an unsettling intensity. Fear washed over the two men, their minds racing with questions of the children's intentions and the reason they had become pawns in this nightmarish game. The silence hung heavy in the air, broken only by the distant sound of the witch's wings above. It seemed as though time itself had come to a standstill within the confines of the circle.

Thiago and Raul exchanged worried glances, their hearts pounding in their chests. They knew they had to find a way out, to break free from the clutches of the encircling children. But the circle remained unbroken, sealing their fate within its ominous boundary. In that harrowing moment, the children's intentions remained a mystery, their motives shrouded in darkness. Were they mere pawns, manipulated by the witch's dark influence, or did they harbor their own malevolent agenda? The air grew heavy with anticipation, as if the very essence of the night had conspired against them. They could almost feel the weight of their desperation, their fight-or-flight instincts urging them to find an escape from this surreal nightmare.

As the children halted their advance, the witch continued to circle above, her presence casting an eerie shadow on the ground beneath. Thiago and Raul felt their minds racing, trying to make sense of the unfolding events. The air crackled with tension as they braced themselves for what awaited them within the ominous circle. To their bewilderment, two of the children parted, creating an opening for a figure to emerge from the darkness. It was Ben Hamilton, the gravedigger. His haggard appearance and disheveled attire only added to the sense of unease that gripped the two men.

Ben stepped forward, his pensive eyes filled with an unspoken purpose. The moonlight played upon his face, casting haunting shadows across his features. Thiago and Raul exchanged wary glances, unsure of Ben's intentions. In that moment, silence enveloped the scene, broken only by the faint rustle of leaves, the swooshing sound of the witch's wings above, and the distant hoot of an owl. The air felt charged with anticipation, as if the very fabric of reality held its breath, waiting for the revelation that was about to unfold.

As Ben positioned himself in front of the open graves, two children, Ethan and Chloe, silently stepped forward, taking their places on either side of him. The eerie stillness hung in the air as they stood motionless, their presence adding an unsettling element to the already unsettling scene. In eerie silence, Ben extended his hand, slowly moving it across the exposed graves. As if in response to his touch, a faint tremor coursed through the ground, and wisps of smoke began to rise from the depths of John and Martha's graves. Thiago and Raul watched in mounting horror as the smoke swirled and coalesced, taking shape before their disbelieving eyes. To their consternation, John and Martha emerged from their resting places, their movements slow and deliberate. The couple joined the enigmatic group, standing alongside Ben, Ethan, and Chloe.

A sense of dread encompassed Thiago and Raul as they beheld this unholy reunion. The sight of the once-deceased family now standing before them defied all reason and comprehension. The oil-burning lanterns cast an eerie glow upon the scene, illuminating their pale and lifeless forms.

Their eyes, devoid of warmth or humanity, locked onto Thiago with an unsettling intensity. It was as if the veil between the living and the dead had been torn asunder, exposing a realm of unimaginable darkness and malevolence.

Thiago trembled with fear as he faced the piercing gazes of the vengeful figures before him. Fate had led him to this cursed cemetery, where the specter of retribution loomed for the heinous act he had committed, but there was a truth he had yet to uncover. It wasn't that he took the lives of the Dawson family, but from his lack of remorse and his unwillingness to change his wicked ways.

Amidst the somber realization that he was condemned to face his past sins, Thiago's heart bled for his brother, Raul, an unwitting bystander entangled in the web of his guilt, an innocent soul swept up in the tides of his wrongdoing. The bond between them, forged by blood and shared history, intensified the agony within Thiago's tormented heart. How could he bear the burden of knowing that his actions had inadvertently endangered the life of his beloved brother? Summoning whatever courage remained within him, Thiago pleaded with a quivering voice, his words a desperate plea for mercy. "Please spare my brother. He had no part in what happened. He is innocent."

As his plea reverberated through the stillness of the cemetery, the air itself seemed to hold its breath, waiting for a response from the undead that gathered around him. The Dawson family didn't respond as they regarded him with stern, unforgiving expressions, but Ben, the orchestrator of this sinister gathering, raised his hand into the air, summoning the witch with a ominous purpose. "He's far from innocent."

Thiago's heart sank as he watched the witch descend from the night sky, her talons sinking into Raul's head with a vice-like grip. In a swift motion, she lifted him high above the ground. A gasp caught in Thiago's throat as he witnessed his brother being lifted mercilessly into the air, carried away into the sinister abyss of darkness. The sound of Raul's screams pierced through Thiago's soul, haunting him with a wave of indescribable dread. With each passing moment, Raul's anguished screams grew fainter, gradually dissolving into an eerie silence.

Falling to his knees, Thiago's voice cracked with pain as he cried out to Ben, his words laced with desperation and disbelief.

"Oh my God! Why... why did you do this!?! I told you he was innocent!"

Ben stood before Thiago, his expression devoid of remorse, a twisted smile playing on his lips. His voice dripped with cold conviction as he unveiled the dark truth. "Your brother was far from innocent. He was a merciless killer, responsible for the many deaths of innocent souls. He left behind a trail of shattered lives, countless women violated, and numerous children scarred by his sick desires. I have waited patiently for this moment, trapped within the confines of this graveyard. Your release from prison provided the perfect opportunity to lure him here, to face the consequences he so justly deserves."

As Ben's words hung in the air, Thiago's mind spun, connecting the sinister dots that led to this malevolent revelation. Every encounter, every unsettling event fell into place like a macabre puzzle, masterminded by Ben. From the harrowing encounter with the old witch on that desolate road, to the cryptic guidance of the old woman at the church, the ominous presence of the blackbirds at Luis' house, and the eerie encounters with the children at the motel— they were all meticulously orchestrated pieces of a

101

diabolical plan. Even the apparent accidents, like the backhoe and the manipulated gate chain, were mere pawns in Ben's twisted game, designed to draw them inexorably toward this unholy place for the final, horrifying confrontation.

Thiago started to respond, but his words caught in his throat as he witnessed a gruesome spectacle unfolding before his eyes. Droplets of blood cascaded from the heavens, showering the ground with crimson rain. With his heart pounding in terror, he turned his gaze skyward, only to be greeted by a horrifying sight. Entrails, grotesque and morbid, descended from above, splattering onto the earth around him with sickening thuds. A wave of dread washed over Thiago, his mind struggling to comprehend the terror that awaited him. And then, as if in a nightmare beyond imagination, Raul's lifeless body crashed to the ground before him. The sight was an abomination, a grotesque portrait of mutilation and savagery. The majority of Raul's skin had been mercilessly devoured, exposing the gory tableau of his torn muscles. His abdomen, a grotesque cavity, lay open, revealing its horrifying emptiness. Shattered bones jutted out from his limbs, as if mocking the fragility of human existence. A part of his spine protruded from his shattered back, while his head twisted unnaturally, an indication he suffered a broken neck.

Thiago's anguish swelled within him, threatening to consume his very soul. The unthinkable had unfolded, and in the face of this unspeakable brutality, he felt his sanity teetering on the edge. Grief, horror, and rage mingled within him, entwining to form a maelstrom of emotions that threatened to engulf his very existence. As he knelt beside his brother's broken body, Thiago's hands trembled, reaching out to touch Raul's lifeless form with a mixture of love and sadness. Tears streamed down his face, blending with the bloodstains that marred his cheeks. In that moment of profound loss, an unyielding resolve ignited within Thiago's shattered heart. A vow to avenge his brother's gruesome fate, to unearth the sinister forces at work, and to bring justice to the malevolence that had defiled their lives, took root deep within his soul.

Thiago's focus began to shift towards Ben, his intention to confront him with the horrors that had unfolded. However, his gaze was abruptly drawn back to his fallen brother when he noticed a flicker of life within Raul.

Hope surged through him as he rushed to Raul's side, his hands trembling with both fear and determination. Gently cradling his brother's head, he carefully rotated it, his heart pounding with anticipation. To Thiago's dismay, he beheld the gruesome sight of Raul's face stripped of its skin and muscles, revealing the raw bone of his skull. The grotesque image pierced his soul, filling him with a profound sense of dread and disbelief.

As Thiago struggled to comprehend the grotesque mutilation that had befallen his brother, a new horror unfolded before him. Raul's eyeballs, devoid of their eyelids, darted around in their sockets, seemingly detached from any rational control, then an anguished cry escaped his lips, filled with torment and desperation. "Please," he pleaded, his voice trembling with agony, "make the pain stop!"

The sight was both bewildering and distressing, amplifying the intensity of the anguish that emanated from Raul's anguished cry. Raul's voice, filled with torment and desperation, tore through the air, carrying the weight of unspeakable suffering. Thiago's heart weighed heavy with anguish as he observed his brother's suffering. "It'll be alright, bro." Although Raul's injuries were severe, indicating an impending fate, Thiago couldn't fathom the thought of losing his beloved brother. Yet, to his confusion, death did not come. Despite the horrific mutilation to his body, Raul's breath persisted, defying the expected outcome. He couldn't fathom how his brother was still alive. His body was nothing more than a bag of shattered bones and ravaged meat, only being held together with tendons and muscles. It was as if a mysterious force intervened, keeping death at bay.

Raul's anguished pleas echoed through the air, his voice laced with unbearable suffering. "Please... kill me! I can't take the pain!"

His desperate words tore at Thiago's heart, leaving him with a profound sense of helplessness. His gaze turned towards Ben, his eyes filled with a mixture of fury and desperation. With a voice trembling with emotion, he implored, "Please help him!"

Ben made a subtle gesture with his fingers, and without needing any explicit instruction, a group of children silently approached Raul. With an eerie coordination, they lifted him gently from the ground, their small hands cradling his broken body, and began to carry him away into the depths of the darkness. As they disappeared from Thiago's sight, the haunting echoes of Raul's desperate pleas for death echoed through the air, etching themselves into Thiago's heart.

In a state of shock, Thiago turned his gaze towards Ben, his eyes filled with a mixture of fear, confusion, and desperation. His voice trembled as he voiced the question that burned within him. "Where are they taking my brother? What are they going to do to him?"

Ben's expression remained inscrutable, his face shrouded in a mask of enigmatic calm. "They are taking him to a place beyond your understanding, a realm of eternal suffering. His fate has been sealed, and there is nothing you can do to change it."

"What does that mean?"

"Death will never come for your brother. He will suffer for an eternity within these hallowed grounds."

Thiago's heart sank, a chilling realization gripping his soul. "Are we in Hell?"

"No. You're in a realm between the living and dead. A place of retribution and eternal torment."

As a sense of dread washed over Thiago, his heart sank deeper into the depths of despair. The weight of guilt for his brother's fate pressed heavily upon him. Though he was heartbroken for his brother's tragic end, a glimmer of resolve flickered within him, for he believed that his role in this otherworldly showdown had reached its conclusion. He understood now that his purpose had been to lead his brother to this dreadful place of untimely demise. "What happens to me now?"

"Everything you have robbed from the Dawson family will be reclaimed."

His eyes narrowed in confusion. "What does that mean?"

Upon Ben's signal, a group of children swiftly encircled Thiago. They closed in, gripping his arms and forcefully extended them, rendering him immobile. The weight of their collective strength bore down upon him, leaving him defenseless and trapped. As they held him down on his knees, Chloe, bearing the visible scars of the car wreck, stepped forward. Her left eye was ruptured, her legs broken, and the seat belt had caused internal damage—rupturing her spleen and lacerating parts of her intestines.

Much to Thiago's confusion, Chloe slowly inserted her fingers into the socket of her ruptured left eye. As she carefully extracted the lifeless organ from its place, his gaze fixated on the unsettling sight in her hand. The severed eye dripped with a morbid concoction of embalming fluid and blood, its pinkish hue amplifying the grotesque nature of the scene.

Thiago found himself trapped in a state of bewildered silence, unable to comprehend the supernatural display unraveling before his eyes. It was a scene that defied logic and belonged to a realm beyond the natural world. Uncertain of Chloe's intentions, he wrestled with the unsettling truth dawning upon him: she was simply revealing the ghastly extent of the injuries he had inflicted upon her. Then, to his utter shock, Chloe made a sudden and gruesome move. With a swift and brutal motion, she lunged at Thiago's face, ripping his left eyeball from its socket. The excruciating pain seared through his body as she replaced his eye with her own detached and lifeless organ. A mixture of shock and agony escaped his lips as she skillfully inserted his eye into her empty socket. As if driven by some unknown force, Chloe blinked several times, causing a mysterious fusion to occur. Thiago watched in terror as his eye inexplicably merged with her tissue, not only granting her the ability to see through his eye, but also correcting the wrong he had inflicted upon her. It was a surreal and haunting moment, one that carried the weight of both punishment and redemption.

The macabre ritual of exchanging body parts continued. Chloe, driven by an unknown force, tore open the flesh on her thighs, extracting her shattered femur bones. With disturbing precision, she then proceeded to rip open Thiago's thighs, forcefully replacing his bones with her own. After she placed his bones inside her legs, their torn flesh seamlessly mended, defying the laws of nature.

Thiago's anguished cries echoed through the air as Chloe showed no mercy, persisting in the grotesque exchange of her damaged body parts with his. In an act of harrowing transference, she removed her ruptured spleen, still oozing with a mixture of blood and bodily fluids, and affixed inside Thiago's abdomen. The foreign organ clung to him, merging with his own flesh. Undeterred by the gruesome ordeal, Chloe proceeded to remove her lacerated intestines, once nestled within her own body, and replaced them with his. The sight was an abomination, a twisted reflection of her previous injuries now transplanted onto Thiago's form.

Thiago's pain intensified with each agonizing moment, his body burdened by the weight of Chloe's afflictions. Now whole, Chloe took her place next to Ben as Ethan stepped forward. Thiago's torment escalated to unbearable levels as Ethan, with a terrifying resolve, continued the twisted ritual of exchanging body parts. With each excruciating moment, Thiago's cries filled the air, creating a symphony of pain.

Ethan mercilessly removed his own broken arm bones, fragile and fragmented, and transplanted them into Thiago's limbs. The excruciating agony intensified as Thiago's arms absorbed the shattered remnants, merging with his own battered existence. Driven by a relentless desire for retribution and to make himself whole, Ethan proceeded to detach his ruptured liver and lacerated pancreas, placing them within Thiago's already ravaged body. The exchange sent shockwaves of searing pain through Thiago's being, each organ integrating itself into his system with unsettling precision.

Thiago's anguish reached its peak as Martha, with a cold determination, took her turn to partake in the horrifying ritual. In a bone-chilling sequence, she extracted her shattered ribs, each one laced with agony, and implanted them within Thiago's chest cavity. Unyielding in their pursuit of vengeance, Martha then relinquished her lacerated heart and punctured lungs, transferring them to Thiago's own chest. The weight of her injured organs settled within him, their damaged essence merging with his existence, amplifying his torment to unimaginable levels.

As if the grotesque symphony of pain were not enough, John, the final participant in this macabre exchange, stepped forward. With calculated precision, he replaced his shattered jaw with Thiago's jaw, the broken bones aligning with a cruel sense of symmetry. The transfer continued as he transplanted his broken neck and crushed cranium onto Thiago's trembling frame, the weight of his injuries now burdening Thiago's very being.

Thiago, caught in a maelstrom of suffering, his body a grotesque fusion of the family's afflictions and an amalgamation of their collective suffering, could hardly bear the weight of the anguish inflicted upon him. The depths of his agony seemed immeasurable as he writhed in torment, his very existence a testament to the consequences of his past transgressions. His screams echoed through the cemetery, a haunting testimony to the depths of his torment and the price he had to pay for his past transgressions.

Having completed their sinister task, the Dawson family, now restored and united in their vengeance, approached their graves with a newfound sense of serenity. One by one, they gracefully descended into their respective resting places, the lids of their caskets gently closing above them. As the final echoes of their descent reverberated through the cemetery, an eerie stillness settled upon the once tumultuous grounds. The air hung heavy with the weight of the supernatural events that had unfolded, and a profound silence enveloped the area. The moon, casting a pale glow upon the scene, bore witness to the closure that had been achieved. The Dawson family, their souls appeased by the completion of their retribution, had found their final peace within the embrace of the earth.

As Thiago writhed in excruciating pain, a group of children, their eyes hollow and devoid of warmth, gathered around him. With an eerie determination, they lifted his broken body from the ground and carried him through the encompassing darkness, towards the small mausoleum that once offered a glimpse of hope. As they entered the solemn

112

structure, Thiago's eyes were drawn to the cold, gleaming bronze plaque engraved with his name, resting ominously on the floor. The tomb that awaited him stood open, its depths beckoning him towards an eternal embrace. The realization of his impending fate sent shivers down his battered spine as he begged and pleaded for them to stop.

With a calculated motion, the children gently placed Thiago inside the desolate void, where pain and suffering would be his eternal companions. As his tomb was sealed shut, the haunting cries of Raul, trapped in his own adjacent tomb, echoed through the chamber. Within the confinements of the mausoleum, darkness reigned supreme, embracing the fallen souls and sealing their fates. Thiago's agonizing moans intertwined with Raul's anguished pleas, forever entwined in a macabre symphony of remorse and despair, condemned to endure an eternity of regret within the cold confines of their eternal resting places.

The cemetery, now shrouded in an unsettling tranquility, stood as a silent testament to the horrors and redemption that had transpired within its hallowed grounds. The chapter of Thiago's harrowing encounter with the Dawson family, and Raul's life of crime, had drawn to a close, leaving behind only the echoes of a haunting tale and a sense of the otherworldly that would forever linger in the hearts and minds of those who dared to remember.

The end.

If you have any questions, comments, or advice, please feel free to contact me at wade.garrett.777@gmail.com.

Best wishes,
Wade H. Garrett

Made in United States
North Haven, CT
24 May 2024

52885147R00075